D1743031

CLERKHILL SCHOOL
PETERHEAD AB4 6AX

Titles in the series

The Air Stewardess   0–241–11209–5
The Dustman   0–241–11210–9
The Doctor   0–241–11415–2
The Farmer   0–241–10937–X
The Fireman   0–241–10936–1
The Fisherman   0–241–11414–4
The Hairdresser   0–241–11211–7
The Lorry Driver   0–241–11164–1
The Milkman   0–241–10934–5
The Nurse   0–241–11162–5
The Policewoman   0–241–10935–3
The Postman   0–241–11163–3
The Shop-keeper   0–241–11416–0
The Soldier   0–241–11417–9
The Vet   0–241–11165–X
The Zoo-keeper   0–241–11212–5

The author and publishers would like to thank Alan Griggs and his crew for their co-operation in producing this book.

Layout by Andrew Shoolbred

First published in Great Britain 1985 by
Hamish Hamilton Children's Books
Garden House, 57–59 Long Acre, London WC2E 9JZ
Copyright © 1985 by Hamish Hamilton
All rights reserved

British Library Cataloguing in Publication Data
Stewart, Anne
The fisherman.—(Cherrystones)
1. Fisheries—Great Britain—Juvenile literature
I. Title   II. Fairclough, Chris   III. Series
338.3′727′0941   SH255

ISBN 0–241–11414–4

Typeset by Katerprint Co Ltd, Oxford

Printed in Great Britain by
Cambus Litho Ltd East Kilbride Scotland

The Fisherman

Anne Stewart

Photographs by
Chris Fairclough

Hamish Hamilton · London

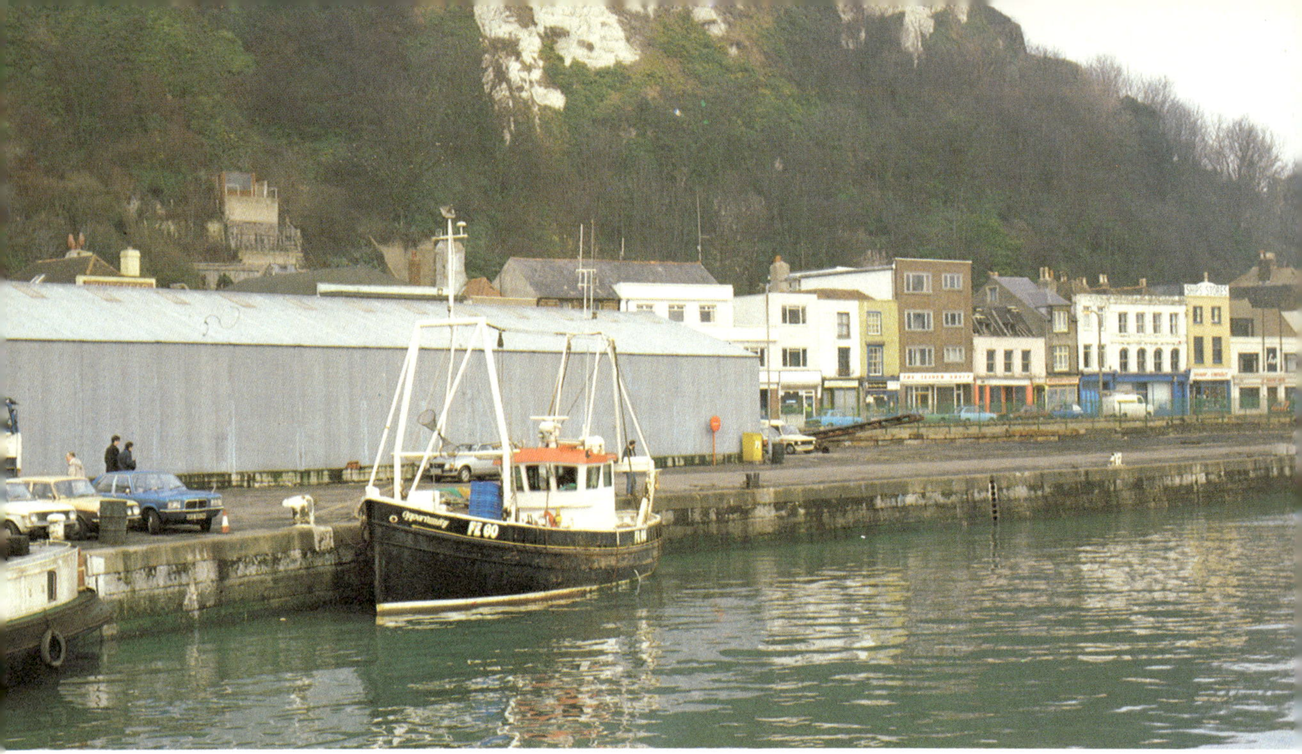
FE 60

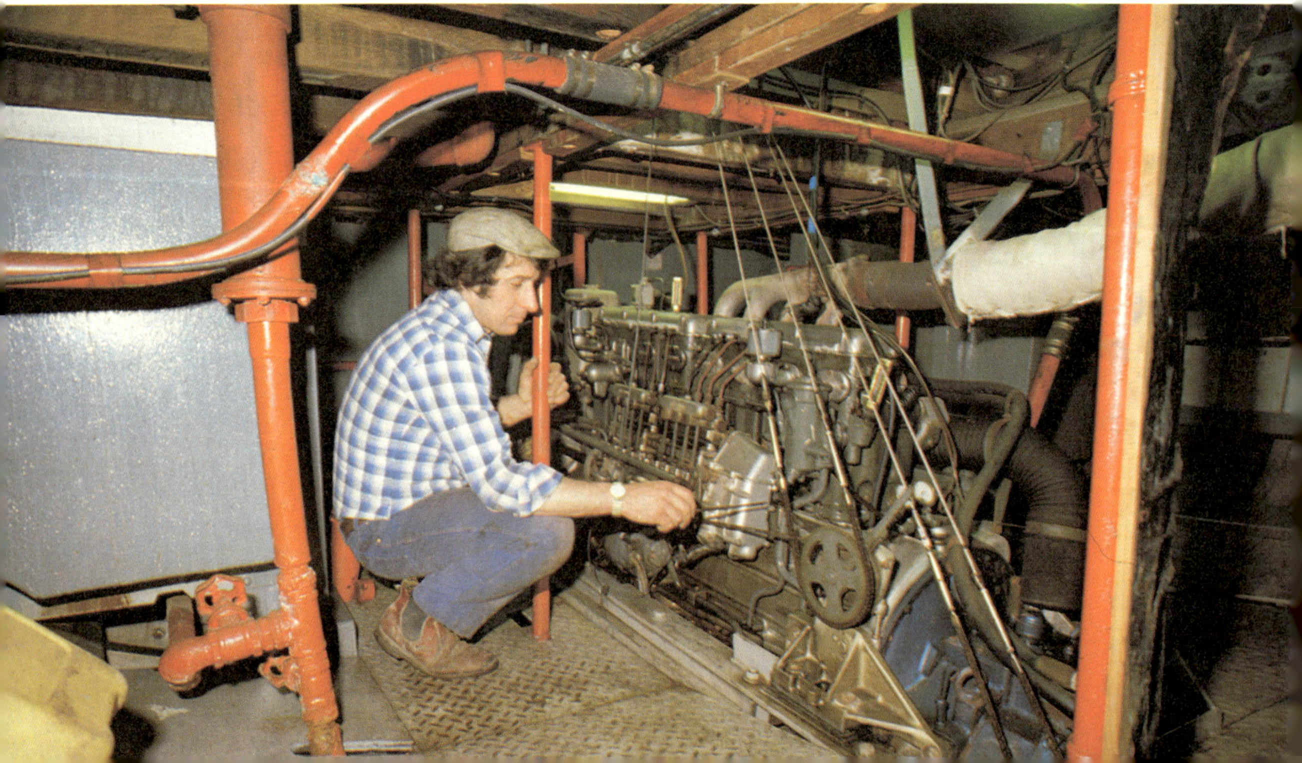

Alan Griggs has been a fisherman all his life. He fishes off the Kent coast for cod and flat-fish, such as plaice, whiting and skate. He usually moors his boat, *Opportunity*, in Folkestone harbour. But this week she is moored at Dover. There are only twelve fishing boats still working from this harbour.

Three or four times a week, Alan gets up early and drives to the harbour from his house in Hythe. When he arrives, it is often still dark. He climbs down to the engine room to check there is enough oil and fuel to last the journey.

As dawn breaks, Alan's crew arrives. Stirling is seventeen and has worked on *Opportunity* since he left school last year. He helps Alan to haul the net aboard. They fold it neatly at the back of the boat (the stern), ready for use.

Meanwhile, Sean makes sure all the ropes at the front of the boat (the prow) are in their correct place. Untidiness on any boat can cause accidents.

Opportunity chugs towards the harbour mouth. Although it is still early, a big cross-Channel ferry is waiting to leave for France. A ferry leaves Dover every few minutes.

The English Channel is the busiest waterway in the
world. And so there are traffic laws here, just as on land.
Alan has to telephone the Port Authority to get
permission to leave.

When he is given the go-ahead, he sails east towards the
Goodwin Sands. There are usually quite a lot of fish here.
The Sands are Alan's favourite fishing ground.

Alan steers from the wheelhouse. It is fitted with special machines to help him navigate and find the best place to fish. Two of the most important are the Decca navigator and the echo-sounder. The first warns him of any wrecks nearby, while the second shows him if any fish are beneath the boat. It also tells him what depth they are swimming at.

As *Opportunity* heads towards the Goodwin Sands,
Stirling goes below to make some tea. The cabin has such
a low ceiling that he cannot stand upright. There are only
two bunks so if Alan decides to stay at sea overnight, the
men have to take turns to sleep.

Sean cleans the windows of the wheelhouse. All boats
must be carefully looked after to keep them seaworthy.
Wooden boats in particular quickly rot without attention.
During the winter, Alan spends most of his time
preparing the boat for the next fishing season.

About 1½ hours after leaving Dover, Alan switches on the echo-sounder. He sees different kinds of fish dotted around the screen. Some are close to the surface of the water, others near the sea-bed. Fish which appear red are specially large fish.

Alan gives the command to start fishing. With the help of a winch, Stirling lets out the wires which tow the net. The wires are made of very strong, thick steel.

Sean lowers the cone-shaped net over the side (the gunwhale), making sure the wires do not get tangled.

The net streams out like a huge string sock. It is over 20 metres long. At the mouth end, the upper edge of the net is attached to white plastic floats; the lower edge is fixed to weights. The mouth of the net is forced wide open so that as many fish as possible will be caught.

The toe of the net is called the cod end. Any adult fish which enters the net will eventually be trapped here. Smaller fish can escape through the mesh. The size of the mesh has been fixed by law so that no young fish can be caught. In this way, the government hopes more fish will grow into adults, which will then breed and increase the total number of fish.

Trawling continues for up to three hours. The men put on their yellow oilskins. Then the engines are stopped and the wires are winched in. First to come aboard are the otter-boards. These are attached to the end of the wires to help keep the net open while it is being towed through the water.

At last, the whole net is alongside the boat. Another wire with a hook is attached to the cod end. A special kind of crane hoists it over the gunwhale. The cod end is opened and the shiny silver fish spill out over the deck.

The men sort the different types of fish into separate boxes. Most are either cod or plaice. They live on, or near the sea-bed. Deep-water fish like these are called demersal fish. They make up over 50 per cent of all sea fish.

Sean and Stirling carry the full boxes of fish to the centre
of the boat. Here they will remove those parts of the fish
that cannot be eaten. This is called gutting.

Nowadays, many big trawlers have machines to gut fish. But on *Opportunity* it is still done by hand.

Using a sharp knife, Stirling slits each fish lengthways and cuts out its insides. He throws them overboard. The seagulls swoop and snatch the flesh before it hits the water. They utter short piercing screams as they hover in the air.

Then the fish are hosed down and packed back into the boxes. There is no need to freeze them because the boat never stays at sea for longer than 24 hours.

This enormous cod is too big to put into a box. Can you imagine how many fish fingers it would make!

The men trawl for another five hours or so. Then it is time to head back to Dover. The boat can only enter the harbour at high tide, so Alan has to time their return carefully. Stirling jumps onto the quay to moor the boat.

The boxes of fish are winched ashore. Today, there are only six boxes.

'Perhaps we should go somewhere else tomorrow,' thinks Alan. 'Then the fish might return.'

Alan drives back to Folkestone harbour. A few years ago, he used to sell his catch at the fish market here. But then the market closed down and Alan and five other boat-owners decided to open their own fish shop. Alan and Stirling carry the fish into the store-room.

When the fish have been washed and checked, Alan carries a box or two into the shop. The rest are stored in a huge freezer to keep them fresh.

Most of the fish is sold to local hotels and fish and chip shops. If the catch is specially good, some is sent to Billingsgate market in London. The shop is busiest on Sunday afternoons when people come for a stroll along the seafront. Many of them stop to buy some fresh haddock or plaice for their tea.

On working days, Alan arrives home at about 5 o'clock. It feels good to sit down after fourteen hours on the go. As Alan and his wife, Marie, drink their tea, they chat about other fishing grounds Alan might try.

'Why not go to Rye Bay?' Marie suggests. 'Jack has been doing well there recently.'

Alan thinks about it. It takes longer to get there, but the catch might be worth the extra time and fuel.

'Let's see what the weather forecast is first,' he says. He turns on the radio – only to hear that there will be Force 9 gales tomorrow.

'It doesn't look as if I will be going anywhere!' he says.

Index

below deck   8
cod   3, 16, 19
'cod end'   13
Decca navigator   7
deep-water fish   16
echo-sounder   7, 10
fish sales   22–23
flat-fish   3
gutting   17–18
otter-boards   14
Port Authority   6
wheelhouse   7, 8